DISCOVER B/
Tiger Cub

Written by Jennifer Boudart

Illustrated by Krista Brauckmann-Towns

Copyright © 1997 Publications International, Ltd.
All rights reserved. This publication may not be reproduced or quoted
in whole or in part by any means whatsoever without written permission from

Louis Weber, C.E.O.
Publications International, Ltd.
7373 North Cicero Avenue
Lincolnwood, Illinois 60646

Permission is never granted for commercial purposes.

Manufactured in U.S.A.

ISBN: 0-7853-2351-1

PUBLICATIONS INTERNATIONAL, LTD.
Rainbow Books is a trademark of Publications International, Ltd.

It is morning in the jungle. Steam rises up from the ground. Jungle plants sparkle with dew. Monkeys and birds chatter high in the treetops.

Look! Three tiger cubs come tumbling out of their dark cave. Today is their first day outdoors. They are eight weeks old and ready to explore.

?

Why do tigers have whiskers?
A tiger's whiskers are almost as sensitive as fingertips. They help a tiger avoid objects, judge spaces, and feel its way in the dark.

The bright sun makes the cubs blink. Their eyes are used to the darkness of the cave. A monkey screams, and two cubs scramble for cover.

The third cub is a little smaller, but much braver, than her brothers. She looks for the noisy monkey.

Her name is Tiny Tiger, and one day she will grow up to be a beautiful tigress.

🐾 FUN FACT
Tigers' eyes work well even in low light, so they are nocturnal, meaning they are most active at night.

A low grunting sound brings all three cubs running. The cubs know the familiar sound of their mother's voice.

Tiny Tiger and her brothers follow Mother Tiger through the tall jungle grass. Their stripes hide them very well. To other animals, they look like swaying grasses filled with shadows and sunlight.

🐾 FUN FACT
Every tiger's stripes are unique! A tiger's face markings are so distinctive that they can be used to tell two tigers apart.

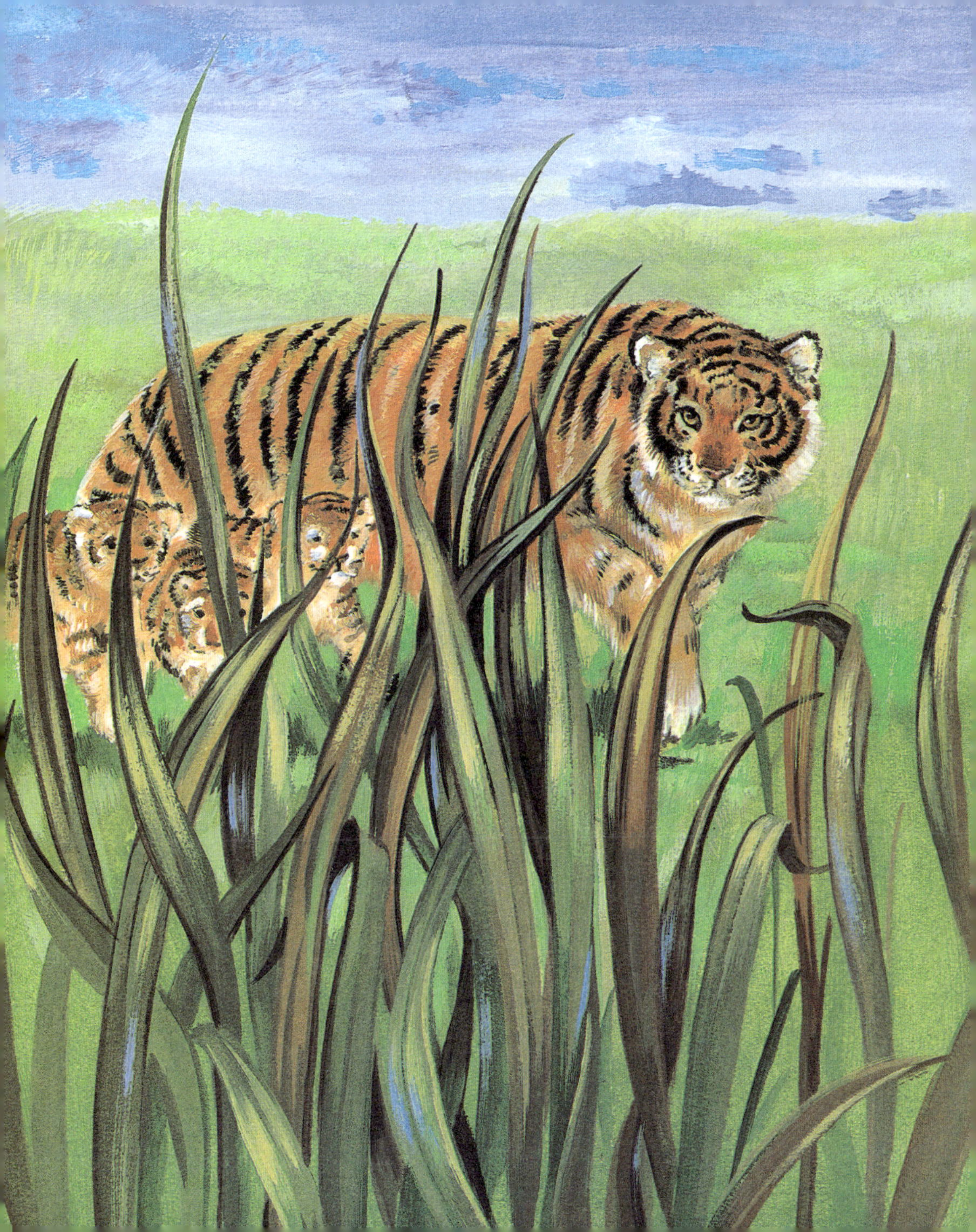

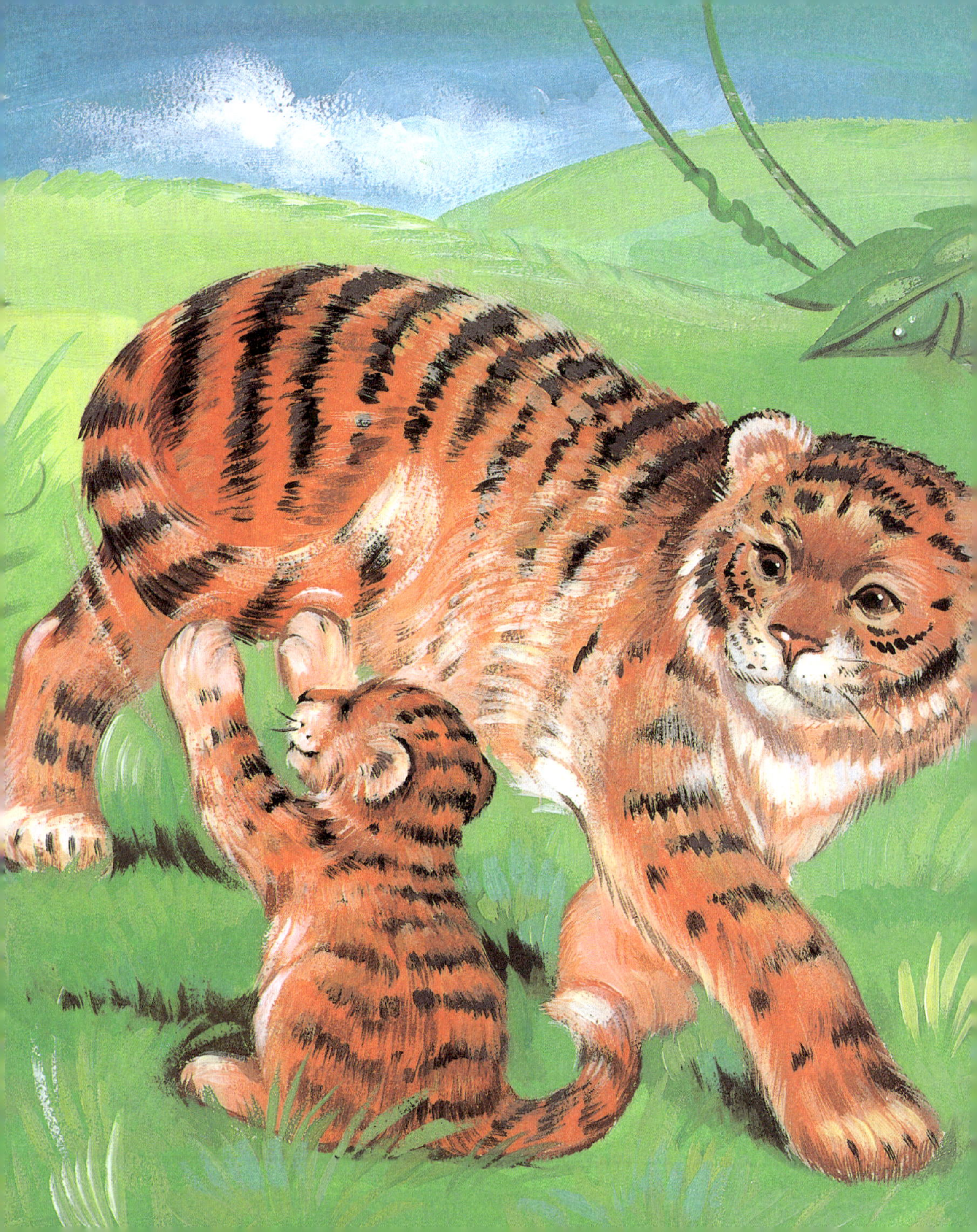

Tiny Tiger is amazed by the world around her. There is so much to see, smell, and hear!

Tiny Tiger sees her mother's long, swinging tail. She tries to catch it! Mother holds her tail high out of her baby's reach.

Tiny Tiger turns to chase her own tail. Round in circles she goes. Her mother grunts softly. Keep moving!

> **? How do tigers keep their claws sharp?**
> Tigers' claws are retractable, which means they can be withdrawn into a cat's paw like a turtle's head is pulled into its shell. Because they are extended only when holding prey, tiger claws remain sharp.

The tiger family comes upon a small lake. It is quiet, cool, and shady — perfect for the hot tigers. First, Mother Tiger checks the area for danger. No jackals or jaguars. Just a few harmless little birds.

The three young tigers have never been swimming. Like all tigers, the three cubs love water. They march right in!

🐾 FUN FACT
Tigers don't like hot weather. They will often cool themselves off by lying in shallow pools of water.

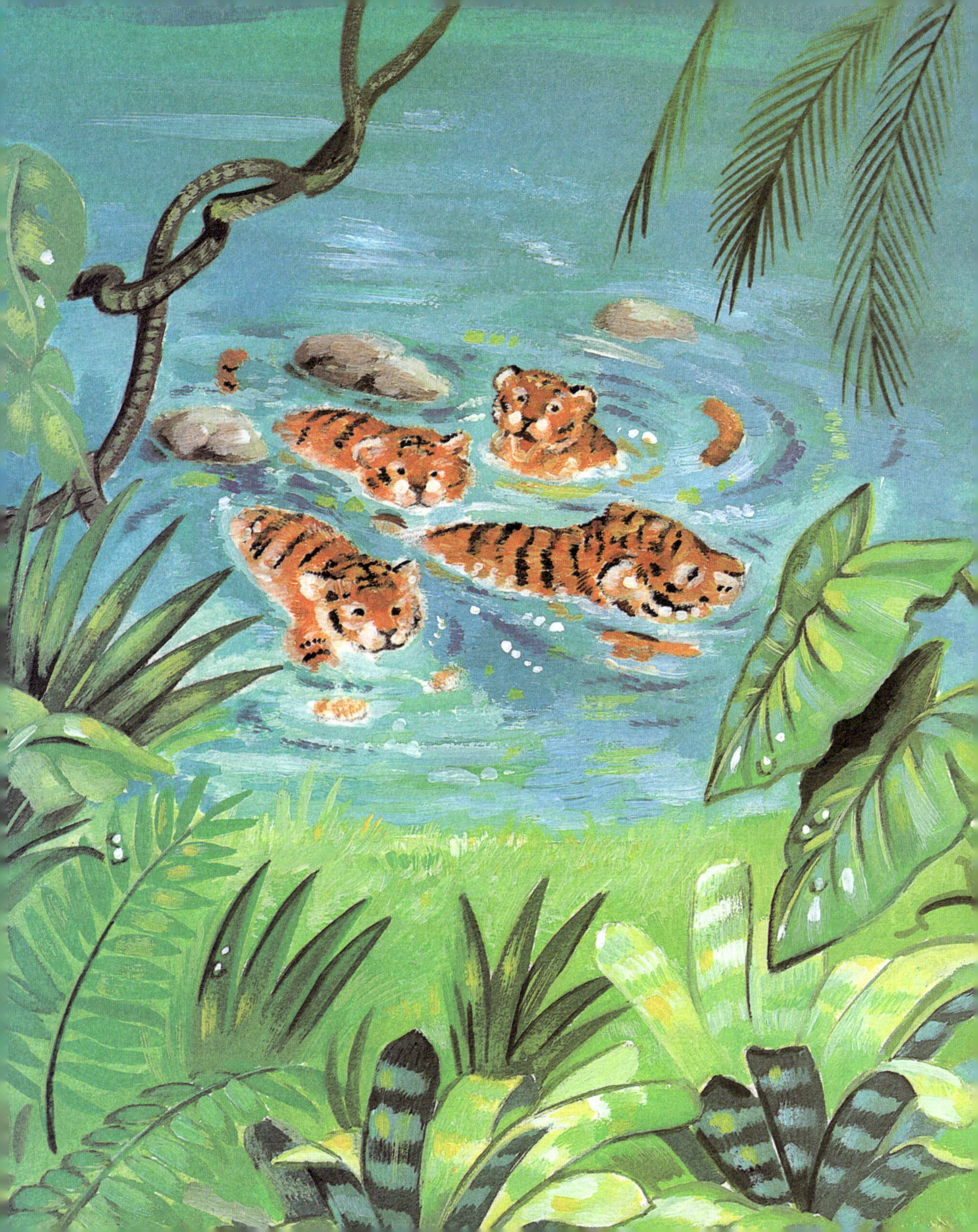

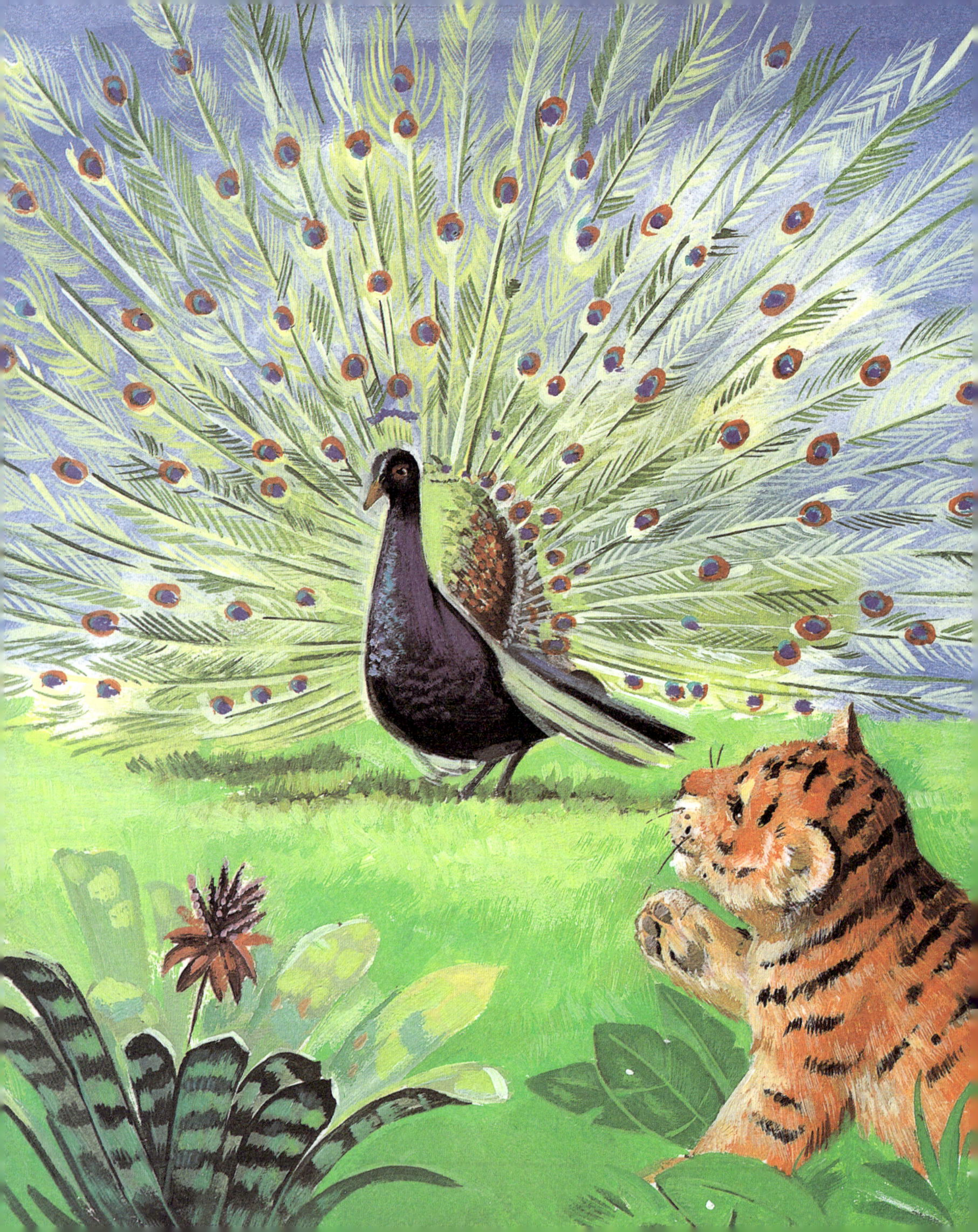

The little cubs wrestle by the cool jungle lake. Tiny Tiger sees a peacock.

She takes a step toward the beautiful bird. It flies away! Tiny Tiger thinks the peacock is afraid of her. She is wrong.

The bird has seen something large in the grass. Suddenly, a loud roar freezes Tiny Tiger in her tracks!

How do tiger cubs learn to hunt?
Tiger cubs play games that are good practice for hunting. They also learn to stalk, chase, and pounce by watching their mother.

There is another tiger here! The cubs run and hide behind their mother. Mother Tiger is not scared because she knows this visitor. He is Father Tiger. They rub necks to say hello.

Tiny Tiger bravely jumps from behind her mother. She growls a baby growl. Her father gently rubs her with his big paw before going on his way.

🐾 FUN FACT
A tiger cub will leave its mother after two years to find its own territory. There the cub will spend most of its life hunting and living alone.

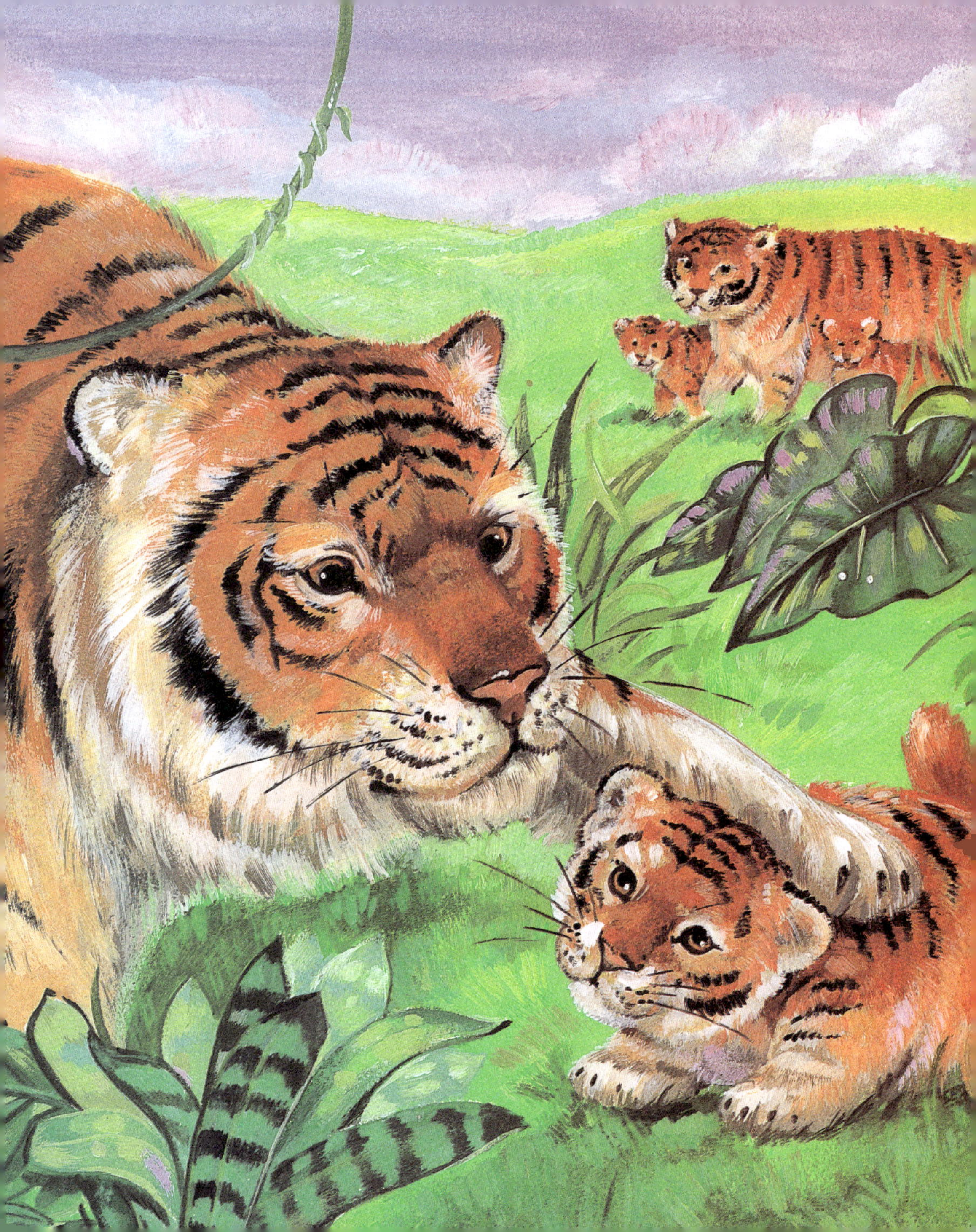

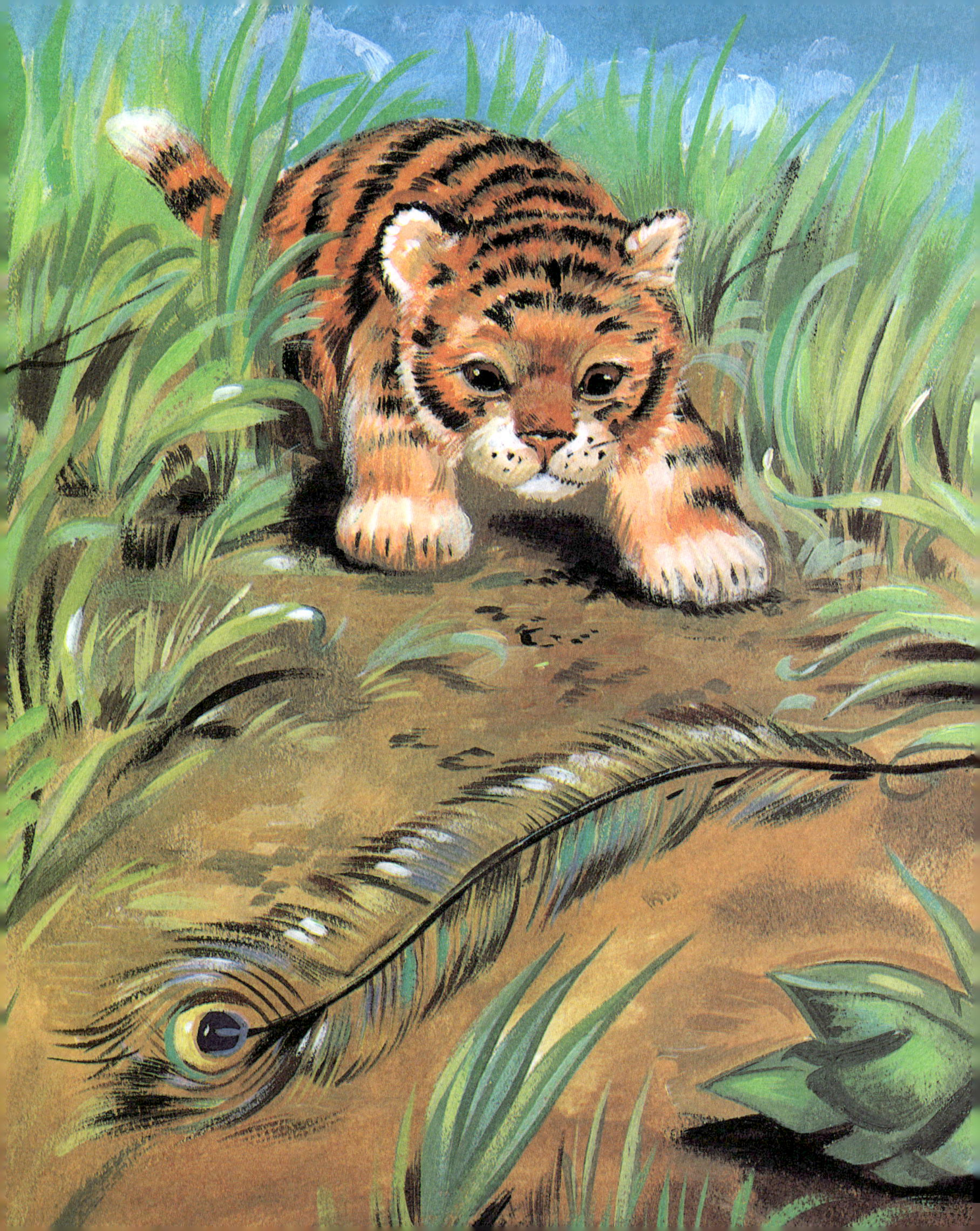

Tiny Tiger is a playful cub. She creeps slowly and quietly to practice hunting. Her little body stays low to the ground, and her ears press flat against her head. Suddenly, she jumps! She has caught a peacock feather!

One day, Tiny Tiger will catch real food. Today is just for fun, though. Her brothers chase her, trying to steal her prize.

?

What do tigers eat?
Tigers are carnivores, meaning they hunt for their food and eat meat.

The family returns home for a short nap. The cubs cuddle together in front of their cave. Mother Tiger washes each of the three cubs with her rough tongue. Then she lies down with them to rest.

After her nap, Mother Tiger hunts for food for her little cubs. She leaves them safely napping near the cave.

🐾 FUN FACT
A mother tiger can carry her cub by gently grabbing the cub's neck in her mouth. Loose folds of skin on the top of a cub's neck are a natural handle.

Tiny Tiger's legs kick as she sleeps. She flicks her tail and growls softly. She dreams of the day when she will grow up to roam the jungle as a mighty tigress.